SMALL TOWN SUMMER NIGHTS

CHICKEN HOUSE PRESS

Small Town Summer Nights

 First Printing: 2023
CHICKEN HOUSE PRESS

Print ISBN: 978-1-990336-44-7

Chicken House Press
282906 Normanby/Bentinck Townline
Durham, Ontario, Canada, N0G 1R0
www.chickenhousepress.ca

Contact the publisher for Library and Archives Canada catalogue information.

Chicken House Press acknowledges the support of *Blank Spaces* Magazine and Pauline Shen for their sponsorship of the writing content that culminated in these final eight stories.

Thanks is also due to the judging panel who selected these eight stories to be included: Haley Down, Barbara Lehtiniemi, Michelle McLaughlin, Joanne Morrison, Marina L. Reed, and Alanna Rusnak

Sonnet 18 by William Shakespeare (1564-1616) Originally published by Thomas Thorpe in 1609 (public domain)

Cover photograph by Jennifer Sharp
Cover design by Alanna Rusnak

Summer's lease hath all too short a date.

William Shakespeare

CONTENTS

Foreword | Marina L. Reed   vii

Not All Sparks Start Fires | Alyssa Bushell   3

Fateful Summer | Casey Fehr   9

The Salmon Son | Daryl Bruce   21

Satan Gets in Through the Cracks | Finnian Burnett   29

The Magician and the Acrobat | Noa Padawer-Blatt   37

Tilt-a-Whirl | Jennifer Moffatt   51

Glass Panes | Crystal Randall Barnett   63

Lulu, Queen Street, Pies, and August vs. Saul, Suzanna, a Chicken Bungalow, and November | Karen Walker   75

About the Authors   88

FOREWORD

I REMEMBER READING MY FIRST SHORT STORY. I WAS stunned by the brevity of the piece. More so, I was stunned by the impact it had upon me. In so few pages and with so few words it left me musing and reflecting and questioning. The mastery of the story was in how much was said between the lines, in-between the words on the page. The words I saw, the words I read, led me to the imagined ones, and it was the combination of the two that wove such a grand and powerful tale. I could see and feel the chill of the evening; hear the haunting silence; taste the bitterness of fear following the main character. Within a paragraph, the author showed one or two characters, but their friends and families and enemies jumped to life in the empty spaces on the page.

The story was alive. And it made me question. Think. Twenty-six hundred words was all it took.

Writing a short story is no small feat.

A novelist can take hundreds of pages to reveal their story and make their characters come alive. Someone writing a short story needs to do that in hundreds of words crammed into a few pages.

To be included in this anthology you would have had to make the decision to dive deep into your soul and explore those zones of discomfort: in order to captivate your reader; in order to bring your character to life; in order to make an impact.

Writing is about putting words together in a way that leaves a reader gasping for breath. It is also about gasping for breath as a writer knowing you have to open those deep dark centres of yourself to find the answers.

It doesn't matter what the subject matter is, a writer's subconscious kicks into gear when not looking. When least expected. And that is when the story becomes magic.

In some of the stories collected here, I strolled in warm summer evening air remembering who I used to be and yearning for who I wanted to become; I cowered as a child at the hand of my overzealous mother who saw evil in everything including her innocent children; I mourned the transition of high school to the next step on the Scrambler ride at the fair; I reluctantly went home again shrouded in mystery; mourned lost loves and wrong choices. I explored and was explored.

It's a fine line between writing too much description that dilutes the purpose of the story and just enough to keep the reader on the edge of their seat, teasing them to fill in the gaps. The reader needs to work because that is what keeps them engaged, keeps them wanting more. It's about showing and when to stop telling. It's about finding a way to wrap things together that gives the reader pause. Not really an ending, but a feeling of completeness, of conclusion. These are the qualities that make a short story sit up straight. So simple, so incredibly difficult, so profound.

In the age of everything technology we still crave the experience of holding in our hands a story that will transport us; that will answer our questions or open new ones we need to be asking. The short story can be vibrant and needed now more than ever.

So don't just read these stories because they are all Canadian, read them because you want a reprieve from a screen. Read them because you want to explore a piece of yourself left hidden. Read them because they are too good to miss.

Bravo to all.

Marina L. Reed
B.A., B.Ed., M.A.

SMALL TOWN SUMMER NIGHTS

Small town: social groups where ordinary people live

NOT ALL SPARKS
START FIRES

Alyssa Bushell

I'T'S A SUMMER NIGHT LIKE A FEVER, STICKY WITH sweat and verging on delirious. Every front porch swing and backyard Adirondack down the street play host to listless bodies searching for some scrap of cool in the darkness. The cool is not forthcoming.

Those who sleep—or try to sleep—twist their sheets in fretful dreams to the rhythm of unbalanced ceiling fans that do nothing more than ripple the humidity into reluctant motion. Those who don't, well, there's no relief for them.

She and I, we sit in silence on twin lawn chairs from our childhood days. They're the same chairs we sat on when our feet could barely reach the ground, selling watery lemonade to neighbours under the blistering sun. Their fraying plastic webbing crackles around aluminum that has barely stood the test of time.

I can count the fraught relationships that decayed long before these chintzy chairs—people coupled and split, come and gone, fractured parts of families up and moved away. Half of hers stayed, and half went, and she'd never really been a whole person since; she looked for love wherever she could find it. I wasn't looking much at anything back in those days, eyes full of baseball and fire trucks, scraped knees and setting twigs on fire through broken bottle glass.

I think we had a chance, once upon a time, so long ago the memories are faint and hazy as the horizon on a late August day. We used to meet on the old trestle bridge after midnight, all hushed giggles and whispered dreams. We'd lie close enough to feel each other's heat—not touching—flat on our backs, staring up at the stars. Sparks flashed between us then, glinting like the fireflies we never tired of watching. But that was teenaged whims and fickle longings and wasn't meant to be.

Most would say that we grew up together, but we grew up at different times, she and I. She married young and birthed herself into adulthood and a world of silent pain. I ran wild and free but wistful, fighting fires by then and feeding on the heady thrill. It always seemed I'd lost something I never had, something that smouldered on within us but never quite caught fire.

Tonight we both stare forward into nothing, parallel, her

and me. The smoke of someone else's campfire drifts between the fence boards, awakening a memory I'd long since locked away. A chorus of cicadas competes with the thump of bass that's more a feeling than a sound from around the corner. The night's alive with sultry summer noises, but still we sit in heavy silence. There's so much left unsaid, but nothing more to say. She had handed me the truth as if peeling off a segment of an orange; it was self-contained, but I know it's not the whole.

Don't tell, she whispers into the night, her voice nearly lost in a sudden burst of beer-soaked laughter down the street. That suffocating night—what other secrets will it hold?

In a town this small, nothing's hidden long. Stolen confidences are traded over coffee or dug up raw to chew on behind the neighbour's back. If they don't know the truth, they'll manufacture one. There were plenty of rumours swapped about her husband before the fire, murmurs of sordid deeds that no one could prove. The building burned and laid both him and the rumours to rest and brought a sort of uneasy hush that lasted.

I'd done my best all those years ago, battling the blaze. It was a night as hot as this one that the flames made hotter still. By the time the sirens pierced the deadly dark, the house was fully engulfed. Three kids he had—they all got out —and that young wife, standing in the street barefoot in her flimsy robe. She had a greyish pallor to her face, and an emptiness behind her eyes that shouted 'I'm a widow' before even the first hose had been drawn. The wee ones' tears ran streaky lines down their soot-smeared cheeks, but she just stared into the flames, oblivious to their cries and the flurry of emergency around her.

Despite the things I'd heard about him, I didn't break through those flames any slower than I would have for anyone else. It's a line that ought not be crossed, deciding who's worthy of rescuing or not. We plunged into the heavy smoke, dizzied by the oily scent of kerosene, but by the time we found him it was far too late and he was gone. A whole life went up in smoke and with it all his sins, nothing left behind but a burnt-out shell of a house and a wife and a town that was all too eager to move on.

The cause had to be investigated, of course. It was quickly ruled an accident and soon replaced as front page news. All the cookie-cutter houses on that street are full of faulty wires and synthetic furniture, and no one blinked an eye at how fast it was all wrapped up.

Instead, the whole town came together—it's just what neighbours do. Church ladies appeared with garbage bags of hand-me-downs and weathered cardboard boxes of appliances intended for the next yard sale. Someone else made offer of a dingy one-bedroom apartment whose previous resident was never coming home. It was only half-furnished, but then she had nowhere else to go. I'd knock around with sacks of groceries from time to time, but my pride back then wouldn't let me show too much interest—the wrong sort of interest, with nothing to be gained by then.

And now I hold a segment of the truth, but what to do? As if I needed in this heat a new reason to perspire. That's the tricky thing about the truth; once given, it cannot be taken back. I'd never asked to know that all along, the thing was not as much an accident as we wanted to believe. Whatever spark had ever flashed between us, her and I, this heavy truth I hadn't asked for snuffed it out, and we were left with nothing but the acrid scent of flames extinguished long ago.

I didn't light the fire, she said, *but I stood back and watched it burn.*

FATEFUL SUMMER

Casey Fehr

THE NIGHT I FOUND THE NOTE, I WAS DESPERATE: for change, adventure, connection. Adrift in a sea of possibility and without a single lifeboat of love or security, I was determined to make a life for myself in this sun-drenched beach town.

I'd been here a month with only a dead-end job to show for it when I wandered into the café. It was trendy in a low-key way. A way that was trying hard not to be trying too hard. Plush jewel-toned chairs clustered around wooden tables that must have been salvaged from thrift stores and yard sales. Enticing descriptions of fancy lattes and homemade baked goods were scribbled on a chalkboard menu. It was a place for intimate conversation, where readers could easily lose a day, a quiet refuge where lonely souls like me could pretend to belong.

I ordered a London fog and claimed a spot in front of floor-to-ceiling windows. Outside, people window-shopped for antiques and expensive clothing in the water-coloured morning light. A stall selling bouquets and homemade jams stood watch over tourists and locals alike. The tea was hot and I revelled in the pain that scalded my mouth with every sip. I wondered at the stories of the other café-goers and lost myself in jealousy. This life was too close to what I had left behind. Moving sixteen hours away from my landlocked West-coast city was meant to give me more than this.

I rose, unable to stand my thoughts any longer, leaving my half-finished drink the way I left everything: half finished, unsatisfied. It was then that I noticed the corner of a napkin peeking out from a drawer in the low coffee table. I yanked it out, my restless fingers ready to tear it to shreds and leave it for the barista to deal with. The urge quelled when I noticed the thick black ink that bled into the crisp white, crumpled but legible. I sat back down, smoothed it out on the table, and read hungrily:

"Camille, I have always loved you. There is nothing that makes me happier than sitting across the table from you here, in our favourite place, on our fifth anniversary. May we always return here, and to one another."

The sickly-sweet words twisted a knife in my gut. I

wrenched the drawer open, wood scraping hideously against wood, to shove it back where it had come from. Surprise and anticipation jolted through me as instead of dusty, empty innards, I discovered a bounty: dozens upon dozens of notes. Some scribbled on napkins like the one in my hand, some on notebook paper or over ads torn from magazines. Some were coffee-stained or age-stained, some crumpled or folded ten times over, while others yet were pristine. I spread a fistful on the surface of the table. *Let them not all be love notes. Let there be one for me,* I begged the universe.

The drawer was a Pandora's box of love, heartache, bad poetry, and stories. A secret treasure trove discovered only by the fortunate few who happened to sit at this exact seat, in this exact café, who happened to pull open a small low drawer. Some were only messy doodles, while others filled front and backs of pages with script.

I was here! - Carmen, Aug. 9, 2015, screamed one.

H.G. you were my best friend. I can't believe you could do this to me. I can't do this without you! wailed another.

Yet another trilled: *I'm on a date with the most amazing woman. She could be the one!*

I could have stayed for hours, delving into the personal thoughts of every ghost who'd sat in my place. At some point, I waved down a passing barista for more tea. I found the pain of the burn less delicious this time, as I feasted on the happiness and heartbreaks of others.

Eventually I swept the pile back into its tomb for the next archaeologist. I kept only one that I knew had been lying in wait for me: A green-penned poem that flowed across half a lined notebook page.

Whatever I try
My soul dies
Nothing but enmity
Sprung from jealousy
When I've grown
Let me not be alone.
J. A. - January 2021

Perhaps not the most sophisticated poem, but I was no literary critic. I only knew that the words reflected the desperation in my soul. I returned to the poem day after day. Read and re-read it. Who was J.A? Were they still alone, six months later?

I dragged myself through the long days, answering calls and making invoices in the dreary, grease-scented automotive office that was so different, yet every bit as soul-sucking as all the other jobs I'd tried. I returned to the note every evening, marvelling at this person who could speak to my true self so succinctly, who could see me without us ever having met.

One such evening, sitting in the low-angled July light with a bottle of chardonnay, my eyes caught the imprint of letters sprawling between the blue lines. I stilled, unwilling to let my hopes raise. It was nothing, I told myself, though already it seemed too much like fate. The pain in those few lines called to me and held a mirror to years of my life. I couldn't let someone else suffer alone.

Fumbling in the drawer of junk generously left by a previous tenant, I scrounged up a dull pencil and sticky note. I reminded myself to breathe as I layered the sticky note over the poem and gently rubbed the pencil back and forth over it with nearly religious care. The words emerged with painful slowness, some more obscured than others, like when eyesight adjusts after being trapped indoors for too long. In that now-familiar sloppy script, I now read:

3 months - 125$
Monday 3:45
Michael Caddel

I sat back, then stood up. Sat down again. This *was* fate. Downing the rest of the bottle, I began to Google.

The next two weeks passed in a blur. I'd drag myself through the work day, then rush to Wolf's gym—the only gym in town and the workplace of personal trainer Michael Caddel. Some days I hid behind a book on the bus bench across the street. On others I circled the block, pretending I enjoyed the stroll. Once I tried the New Age crystal shop across the street, but the clerk's eyes followed me with so much hostile suspicion as I lingered near the windows that I didn't try again.

I studied every passing face, wondering if they were J.A.

Whenever I tried to picture them I came up with a mishmash of ever-changing features. Sometimes tall, sometimes short. Sometimes with brown curly locks or straight raven ones. Sometimes male, sometimes female. Maybe Black, White, or Asian. It didn't matter much, only that they were my soulmate.

After a particularly draining day at work, I was ready to leap. I called the gym and inquired about personal training services. Five minutes later I was scheduled for a 10 a.m. session with Michael Caddel that Saturday.

The workouts were brutal. I'd spent too many nights drinking and moping, using summer and loneliness as an excuse. Whether it was the exercise or the feeling that I was getting closer to love, I enjoyed every minute of it.

My first five sessions passed without much progress towards finding J.A. Michael was nothing if not a professional, and he did not speak much beyond explaining the day's program and the technical aspects for each machine or lift. He did, however, tend to leave his journal with workout notes and schedules for each week open on nearby benches as he coached. With a little patience, it was simple to take advantage of one of his short check-ins with the receptionist to flip a couple of pages back and scan the names of clients: *Paul, Mark, Brittany, Ray, Beth...*

My eyes jumped to a "J" halfway down the page. *Jackson.*

I repeated the name to myself, whispering it like a prayer. There were no last names, and the time slot was different, 2 p.m. instead of 3:45 on Mondays and Thursdays, but it was enough of a lead for now. I turned away from the book and threw myself into the workout with renewed energy just as I heard Michael say goodbye to the front desk girl.

Monday came slowly. Barbecues and yard sales dominated my street as people gripped the coattails of summer, though I stayed out of the fray. I barely slept, though it was more than the heat that kept me up. Anxieties plagued me: it was possible that my J.A. had quit the gym months ago, or that they no longer trained with Michael. They must have as restless a soul as I did—what if they had moved far away? My drinking, which had slowed in the weeks previous, picked up again.

I faked a headache, left work just after noon on Monday, and headed straight for Wolf's. It was dead, being a weekday, and I selected a treadmill where I could watch the door and the front desk computer screen. My heart pounded with anticipation and I had to keep slowing to a walk every few minutes when the fear of fainting overtook me.

Michael waved at me, clearly pleased to see me putting time into fitness outside of our training sessions. A few people trickled in and out, but covert glances at the computer revealed none who matched the poem's initials until nearly 1:50. Finally, a tall, pale man with hunched shoulders and dishevelled blonde hair swiped his key fob and dropped down onto a bench to pull off his strappy leather sandals. My eyes slid to the screen, hardly daring to look. *Jackson Adler* flashed in green at the top of the screen, indicating an active membership. There could be no doubt:

this was J.A. The one who was meant for me.

I mashed the red stop button on the treadmill, counting on my breathlessness to go unnoticed in this context, though it had nothing to do with the exercise. Grabbing my water bottle, I headed out the door and onto my bike without stopping to take off my indoor runners. I needed time to celebrate my success in private and to make plans, I couldn't overplay my hand the first day.

Now that I knew what J.A.—Jackson—looked like and what his training days were, it was easy: cross eyes just often enough in the mirror. Give a shy smile in greeting every time I saw him. Use the weight machine one or two over so that I was always in his peripheral vision.

I started following him home three weeks later. I'd leave the gym shortly before I knew he would, or a couple of minutes afterwards. I alternated between biking and driving, trying to be less conspicuous. The smallness of the community worked against me without traffic to hide in, but I was careful.

Some days I only drove by. Others I crouched under the blue spruce in the backyard, watching through the windows when the sun finally set and I could see inside clearly. He seldom closed the blinds. The pine needles, bugs, and sap that I pulled from my hair daily were worth it.

We spoke for the first time on August 20th.

"How was your workout?" he asked, untying his lifting shoes alongside me.

I smiled the radiant smile I'd practiced in the mirror since starting at the gym.

"I love the runner's highs, but some days all I want to do is sit on the beach with a beer!" I said, sounding nothing like myself. I had to consciously stop from jumping up and down when he told me hesitantly that maybe we should grab one together sometime.

"I'd love to!" I chirped good-naturedly, floating out the glass-plated door. Soon I would have him, and everything would be perfect.

It took him another two weeks to approach me for more than just a passing hello. He was shy, as I expected. Lonely people like us often are. I didn't mind waiting now that I'd found him; I'd already waited twenty-nine years just for this. We set a date for the following Friday, and I began to plan.

We met on the beach at sunset, when the late summer heat had not yet faded from the sand. I had planned it perfectly: a red-and-white striped beach towel. A wicker basket. Two cold beers. A smile on my lips and my prettiest sky-blue summer dress.

He wore khaki shorts and a loose black t-shirt. I could tell that he didn't date much, he was nervous and awkward in a way that held nothing but charm for me. I felt more alive than I ever had, only pretending to sip at my beer. I wanted to be fully aware of every moment.

We talked about where we'd been raised, where we worked, and our favourite foods. Eventually, I turned the conversation to the café on main street. He said it used to be a favourite, but hadn't been in months now that he was training with Michael and had sworn off baked goods.

"I'm lucky I found you, then. If it weren't for your poem we might not have met at all," I said, watching his heavy brows arc higher above his blue eyes.

"You read my poem?" he asked, laughing nervously. "How did you know I wrote it? I didn't think I left my name. I was in a dark place, I just needed an outlet..." he trailed off, confusion bleeding into horror as I withdrew the knife from the basket.

It pained me to see his distress, but it would only be momentary. I didn't hesitate, offered no moment for him to deny our destiny together. I had found my soulmate, and our souls would be together forever, never alone again.

THE SALMON SON

Daryl Bruce

IT'S ONE OF THOSE BLISTERING, STICKY JULY nights when even the shadowed clouds of early morning fail to quell the pervasive dampness. Like a needy lover, the moisture clings possessively to the air, smothering it. It's the type of summer night that sear the man's memories of childhood, when the house was still as if holding its breath— that stillness broken only by the rattling of the old box fan echoing against the bedroom walls, and the droning of the cicadas in the old maple outside his window.

Through the large windows of the MacGregor's Gas and Convenience, he's momentarily transfixed by the solitary streetlamp shining above the tiny parking lot. Light ripples and dances under the onslaught of muggy heat, rupturing the darkness through a mass of skeletal firs that mark the outer boundary of town. They are the same smudged windows. The same rusted fuel pumps. The same tired vegetation. Here, the past adheres to everything, like barnacles to the shell of time.

He grabs a pack of red liquorice. It's one of the few things his stomach can tolerate. These recent weeks sustained only on liquorice, flat ginger ale, and du Maurier Signatures. He's surprised by the queue of people waiting to pay until he remembers it's tourist season. It's not the town itself that's the attraction, but the ocean resorts three hours further east. The town benefits and sustains itself by being the last small dot on the map where one can refuel, use a payphone, or relieve their bladder—the restroom economy of eastern Canada.

The cashier looks over the glasses perched lopsidedly at the tip of her hooked nose, stray grey hairs pasted to her forehead. He knows her, of course, even a decade later. She's still here. Where else would she go? Her eyes study him as if seeking an answer to a question she's too timid to pose. The man knows what she's thinking—there's something about his features. And then there it is, the flicker of recognition. He has been outed—again.

His parents have told him no one in town knows, and they are unequivocal in their view that it should remain so. There are certain words in an isolated place like this that are kept firmly locked behind private doors, echoed only within familial walls. But the man knows people will find out quickly. This may be a backwater, but its residents still get *The Oprah Winfrey Show* and *Phil Donahue*.

The man's palms are sweaty as he hands the cashier money. She balks, stepping back, staring at the bill on the counter. He feels an eddy of heat swirl in the core of his stomach, washing over his organs, his skin. Anger? Shame? He can't be sure. He's being seen for the first time in months. In Toronto, he had become a ghost, one of many, who walk the streets. Once shrouded in the appeal and frivolity of youth, they were butterflies who, at the height of their beauty, had been forced back into the cocoon and emerged putrefying cells—still living, but unrecognizable.

He doesn't bother waiting for the change; he walks out the door to the spritzing of a spray bottle and the pungent aroma of bleach and artificial lemon. Soon enough, the town's inhabitants will know he has returned. Some will be sympathetic, but most, he knows, will feel he has gotten exactly what he deserves. He doesn't begrudge the cashier, knowing she will spread the news quickly. He understands gossip is a prized currency in a place like this.

The man turns the car onto the unmarked road—a road, like so many here, only locals know. The windows rolled down, he doesn't care about the dust or the bugs. Sweat oozes from his scalp, pools at the follicles, slowly slinks down his brow like worms burrowing into softened earth. The breeze does nothing to alleviate the heat. It feels solid, like something pressed up hard against his flesh. The balmy air clips his breath, causing a sudden rattle in his chest. He grips the steering wheel. The pressure bleaches the tan of his knuckles. Every pop in the lungs, every minuscule scratch of the throat, every cough, whether dry or productive, shrouds his mind in a blanket of anxious darkness.

People often believe death is calm. Still. A moment of serene conclusions where the horizon dividing birth and death becomes indistinguishable. But the man knows this to be untrue. Death is an ordeal, he has learned. A process played out over time, not the slow closing of the eyes as the orchestra swells. It's raw and unforgiving. It's deterioration, weakness, aches, odours, fluids. It's a flood of tests and pills and needles and regulated diets. It's the cruel testament to the law of transitory existence, the inescapable rot of what was once young and beautiful.

The road winds suddenly towards Main Street. The man doesn't bother to look as he turns, knowing the only traffic at this hour are the floundering moths lost under the insistent glow of the streetlights. He feels the gnaw of embarrassment seize his belly at the deserted stores barred up with splintered windows and lewd graffiti. The unkempt lawns with more burdock and nettle than grass. Further ahead, a solitary fellow staggers down the uneven sidewalk muttering to no one, his frayed and sullied jogging pants drooping to reveal the crack of his backside. It's only the degradation spreading through the town like metastatic cancer that reminds the man of the years that have passed since he had firmly vowed not to return. This, of course, was before the ghosts. Before his world, before the world of so many men he knew, shifted onto the very precipice of a mortal coil.

The man thinks of the family pictures his mother has displayed across the sad old house of his childhood. Aunts and uncles, cousins, women with silver hair, men with heavy beer bellies. Most he cannot put a name to. Most are nothing more than pale faces staring out from behind the dust of fleeting time, who have no attachment to him other than a shared nose or similar smile. When he was a teenager, he thought these photos were depressing, full of simple people who had accomplished nothing. Strangers who had remained stationary in this forgotten dot on the map because it's what their parents had done, and their parents before that. To remain steadfast in stillness was bred into them. He was different. He was the first to leave, and subsequently, the first to come back.

Since reoccupying the same room where he once spent sleepless nights dreaming of the big city, a big city full of men like himself, unafraid and proud, the man has become mesmerized by one photo in a chintzy black and chrome frame. It's an image of him with his grandfather, taken when he was about 15. Every time he studies it, he's disconcerted by the young man who stands there smiling at him with his thick, jet-black hair combed back, emulating John Travolta's iconic look in *Saturday Night Fever*. His lips, velvety and pouty. Brown corduroy jacket, an oversized collared white shirt, the top buttons undone to reveal the first stirrings of chest hair, and tight jeans that flare out at the ankles and made his lean, muscular body look an ode to the impeccable tailoring. More than a decade later, it's nearly impossible to believe he and this boy were the same person. Illness does that, the man now knows. A sharp reminder that health and vitality are like the clothing in the photo—a fad that no one will remember in a few short years.

It is not just the unblemished beauty that stands out to the man, he remembers the day the photo was taken. A sunny afternoon down at the river behind the house. Between the two of them, a record catch. The first salmon caught in the river for over fifty years. The hook pushes the catch's mouth back into a bloody, weary half-smile, making the man wonder if it had willed itself to be caught, rescued from the muck of a desolate, forgotten river. He knows salmon return home to the waters where they were spawned to die. Perhaps having swam through the waters of the world, this poor salmon had come home to find love and the acceptance of family, only to find that was now out of reach. That hope probably died when he left his native waters to find the freedom of calmer seas. The river has become a place to die, surrounded by others, but ultimately alone.

The man parks in front of the rose two-story. The house, listing slightly to the left, looks as though it's slowly being swallowed down into the earth. A breeze carrying a few tiny chips of paint from the rotting porch banister swirls in the beam of the headlights before swiftly vanishing when the man turns the key, shutting the engine off. He takes in the view for a moment, trying to remember what it all looked like on that day with his grandfather, when the roof was pristine, and the front stairs didn't sag. When his mother tended to the garden and his father tinkered in the garage. When life seemed gentler, less dangerous. Less brutal. Full of promise.

The man remembers feeling guilty that evening as the salmon lay on a peeling red picnic table, gutted. Its head, wide-eyed, discarded on the ground. He wasn't naïve. He knew that all their meals were slaughtered in such a manner, but he'd never seen anything killed before. His grandfather scolded him to be a man about it and said, *Life be nothing more than sitting around waitin' for what be next. Death, my boy, it's the only certainty, the only thing you can bet your last dollar on. At least now, the fish has got the waitin' over and be servin' a purpose.*

The heat in the idled car is overpowering. The man grabs the liquorice and exits without bothering to lock the door. Perhaps his grandfather was right, perhaps that salmon had served his purpose. But what about the man and the other ghosts being cut down while they should still be living, should still be waitin' to find their purpose? He climbs the creaking steps hoping he doesn't wake anyone up.

Here he is, the salmon son–home.

Small town: provincial or unsophisticated

SATAN GETS IN THROUGH THE CRACKS

Finnian Burnett

MAMA WORKS NIGHTS AND SENDS US TO Mrs. Bloom's for dinner and sleep. On the hottest nights, Mrs. Bloom lets us drag sleeping bags to the screened-in porch where we fall asleep listening to the peepers, the owls, and a scratchy growl Benny thinks is a monster. Mrs. Bloom's toothless boyfriend, Tank, says it's just a mama badger clucking at her babies.

Benny stops under the badger crossing sign and asks if I think we'll see a badger tonight.

"No, Benny." I take her hand to keep her moving. We never see badgers. We never see anything good—just deer most of the time, and sometimes yellow-bellied marmots if we go outside early enough.

Benny wrenches from my grip and drops to her knees behind the bumper of Gordon McNabb's van, the big tan one with a spray-painted naked lady on the side, the one Mama says we should never get in because old Gordon's full of sin and so is his van.

"Come on from there," I hiss. But she's half under the bumper and she screeches like a baby monkey when I grab her leg.

"Stop, Lainey," she yells, kicking back. I squat on the driveway behind her, looking around for either Gordon or Mama, not sure which one would be worse.

"Benny," I whisper through gritted teeth, "If you don't come out from there—right now—I swear to God I'm telling Mama."

Don't swear to God," she says. "It's a sin." She scrambles out and jumps to her feet. Her knees are pitted with gravel and dirt. I send up a quick prayer of thanks that we're on our way to Mrs. Bloom's and not home, because Mrs. Bloom will wash Benny's knees with a warm cloth and maybe give her a popsicle. She'll let Benny put on pants, pants that Mrs. Bloom's only son used to wear when he was little, so she doesn't get dirty running around outside.

"I found a Data," Benny squeals, holding up a hard, plastic figurine, half-covered in mud. It is Data, one of her favourite *Star Trek* characters—I guess. It's hard to tell through the mud, but the yellow and black Star Trek uniform looks about right and if anyone would know, it would be Benny.

"Can I keep it, Lainey?" She stares at me, eyes solemn. "Please."

It's the devil, I can hear my mom saying. Everything is from hell if you listen to our mom. Starships, phasers, television, Tommy Decker from down the street, Gordon's van, Gordon, frozen food, braces, medicine, wearing pants. *Satan gets in through the cracks left when we sin*, Mama says.

I take the Data figure and rub some of the dirt off with my hand. "You can keep it, but you can't tell Mama," I say, handing it back to her.

She takes it and holds it to her cheek. "I can't wait to show Tank."

Mama doesn't know we watch *Star Trek* at Mrs. Bloom's house after play time, when we come in from running in the yard. Before we come in to watch *Star Trek*, we look for animals in Mrs. Bloom's big back yard that butts up against Crown land and has a river running through it.

Tank swears there's foxes and badgers and flying squirrels and coyotes right in their own backyard. Some nights, he comes out with us and builds a fire in the big pit, and as the sun goes down, he tells us all about all the animals he's seen on his camping trips—like bears and moose and even a wolverine once.

As we search for animals, Mrs. Bloom sits on her porch and smokes, smiling over us, only calling us in when it's full dark and we're covered with mosquito bites. She makes us frozen dinners—Tank's favourite—even though Mama sends us with peanut butter sandwiches because she's not paying extra for Mrs. Bloom's food. We watch *Star Trek* with Tank who loves Mrs. Bloom even though she and Mr. Bloom, who lives in Alberta, are still married. We love Tank, even with his missing teeth that he swears he lost fighting a wolverine. He works at the plant and has a tattoo of a motorcycle on his bicep that moves when he flexes, like when he shares his cherry cobbler with me.

Mama says tattoos are from the devil. She also says Satan loves complainers when we whine about being hungry, when we tell her she's hurting us, when we cry about wearing hand-me-downs at school. Mama says Jesus wore hand-me-downs and aren't we a couple of ingrates. Her fingers leave uneven trails of bruises on our arms. Mama's anger flares when we talk about Mrs. Bloom, so we don't talk about her, and instead, we wait for her to sleep so we can go to our room and whisper about the show we watched at Mrs. Bloom's.

Benny skips along next to me, swinging one arm, the other holding Data to her face. At times, she holds him away and looks at him, beaming. I wonder if she's old enough to remember the time when Tank bought her a Captain Picard figure and how Mama screamed when she found it, cursing that Benny must have done something unspeakably bad for Tank to get that toy and how I said the only person who ever tried to touch us that way was her preacher and how Mama beat me so hard I couldn't go to school for a week.

"Just please don't let Mama find it," I tell Benny again and she looks up at me, sad and silent. She gives a nod and I think, S*he remembers. How could she forget?*

On Sundays, Mama doesn't go to work. "It's a day of rest," she says, but it's not. We go to church, and they give us a box of food. When we get home, we pray, and Mama reads the Bible and reminds us that sin is everywhere, even in little children. She inspects our fingers and stares into our eyes. Sometimes, she sees something she doesn't like so she gets out the belt. *You have to squash the sin before it starts*, she says. We eat rice and beans and open dented cans that other people have donated. Sometimes we eat spaghetti with lima beans. Sometimes it's canned potatoes and tomato soup.

Benny runs up the stairs of Mrs. Bloom's house and pounds on the door with one hand, the other still clutching her treasured Data figurine. She runs to Tank as soon as Mrs. Bloom lets us in and shows him the toy. "That's a good one," he says, with his endearing missing-tooth grin. "Data's my favourite."

"Mine too!"

Tank teaches me to play cards while Mrs. Bloom cleans Benny's knees and washes her new toy. She lets us go outside with Tank to look for animals and, in the dusk, right before Mrs. Bloom stubs out her cigarette, Benny spots three moose on the other side of the river. Mrs. Bloom slips quietly from the porch and Tank puts his arm around her. We pull closer to them, Benny and I, holding hands, and we watch Mama moose and her babies. For a moment, I dream about running away to live here with Mrs. Bloom and Tank, but Mama would know where we were, here where Satan comes in through the cracks. When the moose family leaves, Tank puts his hand on Benny's shoulder and tells her that in *Star Trek*, no one goes hungry, and no one ever hurts little kids. Never.

THE MAGICIAN
AND THE ACROBAT

Noa Padawer-Blatt

SHE FINDS HIM IN THE WATER UP THE mountain ridge where birds go to die. He is a halo of feathers when she pulls him out, a bright red leotard stretched over his skin. Half the men from town have at one point thought he was a bird and tried to shoot him down.

They are not malicious, she was assured by the same men when she first arrived, but when he appeared in town eight months ago with no memory, they could not trust him. No money, no family, no one to vouch for him—the rest is belief, and they do not have that.

She has briefly seen him tending to the twelve horses on

the other side of town, the small barnyard room he dips into before crossing town each night to disappear up the ridge.

The mud sags beneath them now when he brings himself to his knees. She sees the writing then, the ghosts of words on his hands and running up into his sleeves.

ACROBAT.

"You know, you can't trust your life with those words," she says.

"Why not?" he asks her.

She reaches forward and pinches open air behind his ear, plucks a coin from nothing. He catches it in a palm still wet with feathers.

In the 1870s this place was cowboy bedrock, a New Mexico block imprisoned in its own myths of outlaws and gangsters, and before that, the Pueblos, the Apaches. The slaughters.

Even if the summer months today cull nothing more than lowbrow tourism.

In a way, the locals say, it is not a surprise that an amnesiac acrobat found his way here. And a magician, like herself, here to cultivate her greatest magic trick.

She rents a room in a ranch house away from the centre of town and falls asleep to the barks of the German shepherd in the basement beneath her bed. She turns in the summer heat. When she fails to stay asleep, she ties keys around her wrist and leaves through the window. For an hour she wanders through the dark acres of land and growing fruit before finding the road.

Without seeing much she climbs the mountain ridge until she makes her way to the water. "Magician?"

He is standing beside a tree, his leotard stitched up in clumsy lines by his shoulder. "Hello," she says to him.

He smiles, tucks his fingers into the fabric by his neck, and shows her the coin. She tells him to keep it and he tucks it back in.

Over time they learn about each other.

By day he tends to the horses and they rarely cross paths. Sometimes she will pass by and see him brushing them, taking them for walks by the rope around their mouths.

It is not so bad, he tells her when they meet at night high up on the ridge. He likes the horses and even though his room collects the desert dust, the rancher is old and aloof and gives him a room and food. He can stay out of the locals' way there.

Still, she is careful with questions about how he got here and why, about his recollection of his early life. All he ever does is smile and shrug; maybe he had an accident that damaged that squishy part of his thalamus. Maybe he has a family out there, a pretty acrobat mother and father.

One local tells her that years ago they swear they had seen his face in a travelling circus, a tiny boy walking on his hands across a yard-long silver wire.

"But who knows, all little boys look the same. You can never be sure."

He keeps a notebook for these types of things, but

whenever she asks about it, he says there are more interesting things for them to do than smell the mildewed pages of his journal.

It frustrates her, and she will try to look closer, for some sort of outrage she thinks he should have.

It relieves her too. She does not press. And he will smile once more, and she will wonder if he might feel a little sadness at how easily she acquiesces.

The acrobat asks her many questions about herself too. He wants to know where she has been, what kind of people she votes for, what she believes in. He wants to see her room in the ranch house. Her room that is plain, she tells him, the only things in there a mattress and her magician's tools, a toothbrush.

And in his hunger to know she witnesses the colourless divisions of her own life.

Before this, the eastern steppe of the Great Plains, down into Baton Rouge, the Bayou in Louisiana. Places that she is sure were beautiful but hold no contours, no real emotion or definition or meaning.

And before that, Atlanta, a fanatic hunter father, a mother too, presumably—who skipped town with a tall red haired man from Norway before she ever knew her face. And a brother, Jason, who died when she was 9.

She feels guilty, of course, for having so much to share and remembering but resenting all of it, exciting in it, all the same.

He feels guilty too, knowing that any form of companionship is an exchange of information—competing childhood traumas, sexual power, capital about how many books someone has read, if they attended school and which one, where they have been and what they have seen and how their palate has changed because of it, and, at the end of the day, stories—of which he has none.

She convinces him to swim with her, convinces him to meet him in the wheat fields, the nearest summit. In the dark they grasp at corn stalks which she makes vanish.

She watches his face turn sparkly with amazement.

"I like that you never ask me the secret. It keeps me— "

" —Humble?"

"Honest. Believe me, the secret is unremarkable."

He bends backwards in his red leotard and tests the stability of his wrists, elbows, then lifts his legs.

"You know, the point of a lie is that you don't know you're being lied to."

"You think I'm lying to you?"

"It would make no difference to me."

And then he walks on his hands. This calms him, he says, so he must have been doing this since he was a child.

And they also talk about aimless things.

They talk about elephants. He loves elephants and believes they are important to him.

They talk about the stunning places she has seen on hunting trips with her father before he went north for the deer.

She has never held a gun, she always says. She has never

hurt an animal, she never will.

That is good because he loves elephants and could never imagine them hurt.

And on and on.

Still, sometimes when they are roving the wheat fields or climbing the summit, he will find her staring at him. He will wonder if his amnesia is showing, his perpetual putting together the pieces and longing for the exact set of eyes and nose, chin and mouth of his parents which inevitably unstitch themselves. He will wonder, if he grew up in a circus like the rumours go, what kind of childhood a circus was, if he felt more unusual and cast off than he does now— he doubts it. And then he will see her frown before continuing the climb, and will know that there is sadness she senses in their companionship because she must figure his isolation excruciating. His rejection by the locals even sadder, pathetic even, because despite their resentment, he still loves them.

They even go into town some nights, away from the water so he can practice on flat ground. The children challenge him to handstands and triple doubles from the bodega patio. They gather around him, flaming out the dying light.

She likes to step inside the old Western-style restaurants with draped beads and hot beer to cool off. She practices too. She sits and hates herself for not being able to think beyond anything that has already been done.

"Magician," a man calls over from the bar one night.

"Show me a trick."

She pulls out her deck of cards.

Afterwards, he asks, "What's the secret?"

She shakes her head.

"Bravo," he says. "I heard what makes a good magician is what makes us all happy fools." Outside, the children cheer for the acrobat.

The parents peek between their shutters and drag their children to bed.

Then there are nights he comes with dark bruises. She says those cannot be from his acrobatics. He only shrugs.

In town, her neighbour says every few weeks some of the local boys corner him behind the butcher shop, try to stuff him in the industrial freezer, torture him with questions his mind cannot answer. But the acrobat always eases their anger with his graceful body, his performance no others can seem to match.

As a child she enjoyed outshining people. She used to steal light bulbs from the houses of her friends and plant them in her backyard. Her father had been so easily angered back then, but she had always been persistent, and when the sun fell away from the sky, the lightbulbs levitating, flickering a dozen shadows onto their plain garden, he had pulled out his rattan chair without a word.

Even when she had told him about the magnets, grown bored by her own secret, her father had covered his ears and sat watching the garden for hours, thinking about his next hunting trip.

She loved her father then, and hated him too. For giving in to her illusions and always looking for something more. A desire so deep he shattered everything she had been trying to do, to put their life back together after Jason died.

Three days before she left Atlanta, he had already become obsessed with the deer. She became obsessed too, a different way.

Late in July, the child of a wealthy tourist wanders up the mountain ridge and gets stuck in one of the trees. The girl is up there for two hours before the locals give up trying to scale the indomitable trunk and point the tourist to the magician, asking for the acrobat.

He is in plain work clothes when she finds him. She is shocked by the smell of the horse barn, but he does not seem to notice, knelt over to clean the dirt from hooves. He looks up, grabs his leotard, and she brings him to the ridge.

The tourist explains what has happened as the locals watch warily from afar, some closer, angry at the acrobat out of habit.

He climbs the tree like a dream. She is always enchanted.

"You look like a bird," the child says when the acrobat gently pulls her into his arms.

He smiles and then hands her to the tourist. He says the girl has a good imagination. The tourist does not look at him but hands him a stack of cash anyways.

The locals are tense from where they have been observing, but some, the pharmacist, the hotelier, the sunburnt mothers, are looking at him with something like faith in their eyes.

He remembers his first month here moving into the small barnyard room with its single overhead fan and faded paisley walls, the rancher taking one huge sniff and grunting as if apologetic before letting the screen door slam behind him. He knew he should have slumped to the floor, feeling the isolation encroaching in its blackness, asking himself how he got here and how any of this could have happened, trace the muddy horse prints and think, filthy, sad, world's end.

All he could feel was his body heat with relief. Could see his first employer who was already such a comic character. His first place that was his, empty but ready to be stockpiled with whatever people cluttered their first place with, mints, art, paper weights if he wanted, which was more than he thought he could ever have just weeks before, the world so pale and unknown, he walked to the water just to see himself change colours, turn blue.

When the acrobat shows her his notebook she says, "Are you sure?"

The wheat field has grown tall and slight in the dark, and when they lie down, no one can see them, even in the moonlight.

He nods and she flips a page.

His notebook is an old Wolverine comic. Between and around each panel the acrobat has filled the empty space with green ink. He shows her where he has detailed his condition. The first couple pages are like this; guesses about his childhood, a circus, a woman in a leotard without a face. She sees where her own life has been recorded with bold, underlined words dotted by tiny stars.

But for the most part, the comic is exhausted with sketches and instructions of acrobatics, various stretches, estimates of the pain threshold in the ligaments of his hands. Bouts of tendinitis.

Elephants.

"Thank you," she says after a while.

"For what?"

"Trusting me with this."

"Oh." He is nervous, she realizes. "You're welcome."

In the third week of August the local boys come for him. They come at night with string and lighters, planks pulled from the damp shaft of the grain mill. They come hardened the way only boys kept from the magnificent world come.

When she finds him up the ridge they have already beaten him with the planks, tied his hands messy with writing behind his back. His mouth is full of dirt, hair dipping into the water laden with dead birds.

One boy is still beating him, a flickering lighter turning him orange.

She forces herself between them.

"You're crazy," she hisses at the boy still holding up the plank.

The boy's eyes are rabid. Years ago she had seen her father's eyes like this, just before he went wandering the coastal islands off Alaska, seeking a deer population he was certain lived there, but never did.

"How can you not know?" the boy shouts at the acrobat, then turns those eyes to her. "He must know who he is."

All she does is shake her head, pulling at the strings around the acrobat's wrists. She hauls him up.

When she looks at the boy again he has dropped the plank. She does not see the anger she expects, only craving.

"If you could just think back," he says, the other boys beginning to withdraw at his sudden despair. "Give us something real."

"I can't," the acrobat manages.

The orange of the lighter falls away, and they limp off in the dark.

Of course she feels responsible.

In the weeks following the attack she abandons their various places around town for his small barnyard room.

She extracts his splinters, feeds him, buys him medicine with the money he received from the tourist. She updates his notebook with everything that has happened, records his injuries and their progression.

At night, for the first time since she pulled him from the water, he sleeps, and she contemplates her master trick. For hours she stares at the acrobat's still body. Stares at his ceiling fan turn shadowed blades. The oscillating light makes her nauseous. She considers lightbulbs, cards, metal rings, but she cannot put the pieces together, though once she was so certain she could.

She considers the boy holding his plank. Where had she been? Casting dreams, her head turned the wrong direction like her father disappeared into the snowy drifts.

The acrobat wheezes past chapped lips.

She feels responsible. Worse, she feels shame.

The money runs out.

The next night, she finds medicine and a bundle of flowers resting by the barnyard door.

He wakes up in the dark with the fan spinning overhead. Her face comes eyes-first from across the room, cautious, worried, but mostly full of hate. He tries a smile to settle her and she scowls. Secretly, he is relieved she is so angry and it is on his behalf.

He spends hours flipping through his notebook, at points laughing at some joke she has scribbled down between the gruesome stuff or something hidden in the comic panels. At points so embarrassed he drowns his face in the pillow.

Finally, he looks at the flowers by his bed, then turns to her.

"Why did they hurt me?" he asks because he has loved them since they became his first community, his first job—a ranch hand—his first home—this room.

"They wanted to know why you can't remember."

"But they already know."

"They wanted something more."

"They always do. And you?"

"I thought maybe you'd wake up and remember."

It is then he sees his hands where she has written ELEPHANT.

"We don't get a lot of things to really believe in," he says to her and presses his fingers into the letters. "But I get all this."

Later, they would continue to climb.

He would be accidentally shot at one more time in late August, and the locals would take him in, set up a room in the town's single hotel. The pharmacist would come to see him as very beautiful and dote on him for weeks, even though the wound would be only a graze. The pharmacist's daughter, equally as enamoured, would spend her evenings stitching up his red leotard.

She would stay angry for a bit. Beat nails into the plank, planning something like revenge. Eventually she would move on and drown it, watch it go down heavy with metal.

She would remember bathing Jason in his last days and pulling him out of the bathwater, collecting his hair from the drain.

She would have brought him up the ridge and they would have seen the tall trees, seen them go dark, tossing coins into the flurry of desert below.

Small town: where people are generally laid back, and where everyone knows almost everybody

TILT-A-WHIRL

Jennifer Moffatt

SADIE IS MY BEST FRIEND.

Her green eyes lit up when she saw me through the crowd. "Izzy!" she squealed, like she hadn't seen me two hours ago before dinner, like we hadn't been together the entire day at school, same as the day before, same as the day before that. Almost all the days, in fact, stretching back to the first day of grade six when she arrived at our school, all hip-hugger jeans and big city confidence. Her parents wanted 'a simpler life' and picked our small BC town because it was 'close to nature' and had a 'world class' ski hill, although they never actually skied. Worked out pretty good for me at least because we'd been best friends ever since.

Sadie and Izzy. Izzy and Sadie. They go together well, don't you think?

I watched her jump to her feet from where she sat waiting for me on the curb in front of the ticket tent. She darted around a pack of moms clutching strollers and sticky toddlers and threw her arms around me. She was wearing the same thing she wore to school that day—short short jean shorts and her mom's old *Star Wars* t-shirt (original trilogy) —and smelled mostly like she usually did, which is to say a creamsicle, thanks to vanilla deodorant and satsuma body lotion. But now the scent was topped with cocoa butter sunscreen and grease. A few grains of sugar shimmered on her lips.

"Did you already have mini donuts?" I accused her, but I didn't actually mind.

"I couldn't wait. We had salad for dinner." She grabbed my wrist and slapped on an admittance band before pulling me towards the gate. "You can get the cotton candy later. Let's go!"

This would be our last summer together. Well, the last summer before everything changed. I was going to UBC in the fall for Forest Resource Management. It had been arranged for years—I'd live with my grandparents, who were only a few blocks from campus in an adorable bungalow shaded by hundred-year-old maple trees. Sadie was taking a year off. Her grades weren't stellar and she hadn't gotten into UBC. She never quite got around to applying anywhere else.

"Oh, well, at least I can come visit you lots," she'd say as we suffered through our final Calc problem set or frantically skimmed *Great Expectations* looking for quotes on the perils of ambition for our last essay. "I'm sure I can get some time off here and there." Sadie worked a few shifts per week at the Save-On but they were going to bump up her hours come September. (Her mom thought they were bumping them up next week. They were not.) She'd have to save a lot for a car that could make it all the way to Vancouver though. God knew her parents wouldn't be loaning theirs.

Just about the entire town was out for the year-end carnival. We didn't have a lot going on most of the time, especially once the ski hill closed for the year, but the Parent Council pulled out all the stops for this event every June. We'd already had our graduation ceremony and we wrote our last exam today. The final day of school was next week, just to pick up report cards and get our yearbooks signed. You could hear summer holidays in the buzz of the crowd and the shrieks coming from the Zipper—the restraint turned down a little, so close to freedom. I held Sadie's hand tighter.

She was literally hopping along next to me down the main row, eyes shining as she took in the games—ring toss, balloon darts, Skee-Ball. The carnival was her favourite event of the year. She even had a countdown going in her Audrey Hepburn wall calendar. It started in April.

"What rides should we do first?" she chirped. "I say Scrambler, then the Zipper, then Tilt-A-Whirl, *then* cotton candy, so we don't puke it up." There was an incident in grade ten, so she liked to plan these things out now.

I paused and looked around, lifting my limp hair off my neck. "Sounds good. And then the haunted house?"

"If you're brave enough this year." She poked the bare skin above my waistband and I smacked her hand away. It was *one* time in grade *seven*. Smirking, she tossed her hair back with a head flick, a leftover move from when she had long, wild chestnut brown waves that constantly fell into her eyes. She got it cut two weeks ago, chopped right off and buzzed on the back and sides, with this adorable little mop of curls left on top. It was courtesy of Dahlia Wright's older sister, who was halfway through hairdressing school. Well, she was, until she dropped out.

Sadie's mom was horrified. I was there when she saw the haircut for the first time, eyes bugging right out of her head like she was starring in her own Saturday morning cartoon. *Mad Mom.* She put her hands to her cheeks. "Sadie! What did you do?"

"Isn't it great?" Sadie scrubbed her hand over the new fuzz.

Her mom shook her head, wordless.

But I loved it. She looked more like herself—freckles darker, eyes brighter. Girl freer.

"It was *one* time in grade *seven*," I replied to her now, as I am required to do. "And it was only because someone said Adam McSorley was in there dropping real spiders on people." I just cannot with spiders. Sadie knows this. We have this conversation every year before we go into the haunted house.

She laughed, a sound that was quite possibly my

favourite in the world. It started with a squeak, a burst of joy escaping that she couldn't hold back, which was then followed by a surprised peal, like she'd forgotten what was funny in the first place, and was now just laughing at the noise she made. All it took was that squeak and I was laughing too. Got us in trouble a lot at school but I couldn't help it.

We did the Scrambler then the Zipper (my least favourite, although still better than a haunted house with real spiders), then got in line at the Tilt-A-Whirl, giddy, sweating, and starting to get hungry for cotton candy.

I leaned back against the railing and scooped my hair off of my neck again, hoping a cool breeze might come along. Sadie's hair was curlier than ever in the heat. My fingers itched to take hold of a lock and see how far it would stretch out before I let it bounce back into place.

"Liam is staring at you again," she said with an eyebrow waggle, disrupting my thoughts.

Despite myself, I turned to look, immediately regretting it when I saw she was right. Ugh. Not a single boy in this town interested me. I'd known most of them since preschool, and had already 'dated' the least-detestable ones in middle school. I had a crush on Liam for about three seconds in grade ten, but when we went to a movie he tried to grab my boob and that was enough for me. Like please just let me watch Sandra Bullock in peace.

"He's coming over here." Sadie rolled her eyes and giggled. In general, she had no time for the boys, but she loved getting them riled up when the opportunity arose.

I groaned. "Let's just go."

"We can't! Look how long the line is now!"

The line snaked behind us, almost to the cotton candy stand. But it was too late to leave anyway. There was Liam. Not bad looking, I suppose, if I didn't think about how he picked his nose in kindergarten, or tried to cheat off my spelling test in fourth grade. Tall and broad now, more man than boy. I suppose he was someone's type.

"Hey, Iz," Liam said casually.

"Lovely Liam," Sadie greeted him, even though he hadn't even looked at her. "How are you this fine evening?"

"You wanna go on the ferris wheel later, Iz?" he asked, still ignoring Sadie. "When it gets dark." He put a hand between us on the rail, leaning towards me. I leaned away.

I'll give Liam one thing, he's optimistic. Imagine thinking he still had a shot to shoot. "No, thanks. I'm going with Sadie."

Liam rolled his eyes. "Shocking. You can be apart from her for five seconds without dying, you know."

I shook my head and took a step away from him, closer to Sadie.

"You sure know how to charm them, Liam," Sadie piped up. "I should take notes."

His jaw tightened. "Shut up, Sadie. I'm not talking to you."

God, what an idiot. I took a deep breath and said it a little louder. "No thanks, Liam."

His lips curled in what I'm sure he thought was a sexy smile, but it didn't reach his icy blue eyes at all. "This might be your last chance, you know, Iz. I'm leaving for McGill soon."

I bit the inside of my cheek while Sadie fought off a grin. We had a game going. Every time Liam mentioned that he was going to (arguably) the most prestigious university in Canada, we had to respond with increasing levels of shock and surprise, completely straight-faced.

"Oh, you're going to McGill?" Sadie asked, all wide-eyed innocence. "When were you going to tell us?"

I snorted a laugh while Liam glared at her. "I *said*, I'm not talking to you."

"Liam, here's a tip for when you get to McGill," I jumped in. "If you're trying to hook up with a girl, don't be a jerk to her best friend." I slung my arm around Sadie's shoulders. "Bye."

"Whatever." Liam rolled his eyes and stalked off. "Have fun sucking face all night," he yelled back from a few metres away, as if it had taken him a minute to come up with that brilliant rejoinder.

My cheeks flushed. "What a dick," I muttered. For the record, Sadie and I had never kissed.

Sadie squeezed my hand that was draped over her shoulder. "Yup."

We rode the Tilt-A-Whirl twice, arms linked, shrieking. Then I got the cotton candy, pink for me, blue for her, although really, they taste exactly the same.

"How does cotton candy do that?" Sadie asked from her perch atop a picnic table, freshly painted yellow for the season. I was seated on the bench next to her, leaning an elbow on her knee, even though our skin stuck together in the heat. The crowd teamed around us, mostly free of moms and strollers now, getting younger, louder. The sun had dipped behind the mountains, casting the mass of bodies in a divine pink and orange light that was wasted on horny teenagers.

"How does cotton candy do what?" I asked, squinting up at her.

"Just... vanish off your tongue." She held up a wisp of blue fluff and demonstrated.

"I dunno, I guess it just dissolves." I stuck a bit in my mouth and focused on how it was there and then it was not.

"Hmm." She peeled off another puff and gazed at it thoughtfully before she ate it. "Makes me sad how fast it disappears sometimes."

"That's why they give you so much." I reached up and popped a pink piece into her mouth.

She giggled and nipped at my fingers.

When the cotton candy was gone it was time for the haunted house. We stood up to go, brushing our sugary hands on our jean shorts, when we noticed a commotion over by the Tilt-A-Whirl. Liam's crowd was there, puffed up and posturing as they jostled a group of boys I knew were from Leafside, the next town over. I saw a few shoves and a flash of a mickey tucked in someone's pocket. They'd been drinking.

"Ugh, this is why we can't have nice things. Gotta get in a pissing contest at the carnival." Sadie stood watching them, frowning, hands on hips.

I shrugged. "Come on, let's go do the haunted house. I hear they bought up all the grapes in town for eyeballs."

But then Liam saw us and muttered at his cronies. They all turned to glare in our direction. One of the large ones—Adam McSorley, in fact, the spider-dropper—said something, and they started to head over. We were an easier target than Leafside's hockey team.

Sadie saw them coming too. She grabbed my hand and pulled me along behind her, although of course I would have followed anyway.

"Hey, where you going, Izzy?" Liam called after us in a dumb sing-song.

We started to run, nervous giggles escaping. Not that I expected Liam to actually do anything if he got to us—he was ultimately a wimp, and heavens, what would McGill think?—but Adam was a bit of a muscle-head and was already mean while sober.

We ducked behind a cluster of people and took a sharp right between two booths, then doubled back down the next row and made a break for it. The haunted house was in front of us—just a series of tents and tarps cobbled together, but instead of going for the entrance, Sadie pulled me around the back. A tarp flapped loose over a pile of pallets and she hauled me under it where we flopped to the ground, winded. We stared at each other, trying not to breathe too loudly. The light filtering through the green tarp turned Sadie into a forest nymph.

I could hear Adam's voice outside. "Where'd they go?"

Sadie sensed I was ready to giggle again. She clamped

her hand over my mouth and breathed into my ear. "Shh! They'll hear you."

I swallowed another giggle down.

She slid next to me, warm shoulder pressing against mine.

We caught our breath, listening carefully for the sound of caveman feet. It smelled like camping and creamsicles under there.

"Thanks," she said, once it seemed they had moved on, hunting for someone else to bother.

I blinked at her. "Thanks for what?"

"For not letting Liam be a jerk to me."

"Of course." *Of course.* How could I let him be a jerk to her?

How could I leave her?

Suddenly there was a lump in my throat and tears stung my eyes. "I'm gonna miss you so much," I whispered.

"Aw, Izzy-bean." Her hand landed on my knee, giving it a squeeze. "I'm gonna miss you so much too."

Our eyes met. The giggles were gone.

She gnawed at a pink lip. "Did you..." she started.

"Did I what?" My heart was pounding for some reason, beating so loudly I was sure she could hear it.

Her eyes were on my lips. "Did you ever...wonder..."

I can't say who leaned forward first. Maybe we both did at the same time.

When our lips touched it was soft and sweet, like cotton candy and summer nights.

I pulled back.

She smiled shyly. "Sorry."

"Why are you sorry?"

"I… I didn't think you'd—"

I kissed her again. My stomach swooped and spun like it was back on the Tilt-A-Whirl.

"Izzy…" she whispered the next time we pulled apart.

"Yes?" I murmured, afraid that a sudden movement would burst this bubble.

"Would you like to ride the ferris wheel with me?"

I would.

We soared high into the syrupy-warm night air, sugar on our tongues, lights laid out below, hands clasped tight on the seat between us.

Sadie is my best friend.

GLASS PANES

Crystal Randall Barnett

THE FLY DRONING ON AGAINST THE OPPOSITE window begins to thwap itself into the clear pane. It sees where it needs to be on the other side of the glass, but is trapped with its unrelenting thoughts in the living room with me.

Where the empathy for buzzing flies has come from, I don't know. Lately I open doors for them like a butler and release them back into nature like a wildlife rehabilitator.

I flap my arms around this one and open the back door at an opportune moment. A black shape darts outside and glides off into the fading day like the ending of an old Western movie. The fly understands where it belongs now that it knows where it doesn't. This knowledge gnaws at me.

I close the door gently, leaning against the wall to peer out at the dusk gathering around the house. Soft rosy colours powder the sky, and liquid gold lines the clouds. I exhale the air held in my belly and wish that I hadn't agreed to stay here in my hometown for several weeks.

I go to grab a light jacket, but the weather has been so hot and humid lately, I decide to leave it where it hangs.

"Hey, Ma!" I call down the hall. "Heading out for a walk!"

"It's getting late, Nat!" Mom shouts back. "You shouldn't be out in the dark on your own."

I roll my eyes, stopping them at the apex of the gesture, trying to retrain them *not* to do that when I am annoyed. Mom sees it every time. She probably hears them even now from her room, listening to them sliding upward in their sockets, irritation sparking from my coffee-coloured irises.

"Mom—I'm 38 years old! I live in a big city; this is a small town. We know everyone here. I'll be fine."

I hear disgruntled air rushing from my mother in what must be an angry sigh. Somehow, I've become as attuned to that sound as Mom has to my eye rolls.

"Take your phone with you and leave it on. Take the pepper spray too." As a peace offering, I turn my phone volume up, then grab the pepper spray perched on a shelf by the door.

"Alright, I've got them!" I shout. "*Totally* unnecessary though!"

I shove both feet into a pair of cigar-coloured

Birkenstocks and slip my phone into the back pocket of my jeans. I push my limp hair away from my face and step into the fading day. It is a relief to be taking a time out. Caring for mothers with hip replacements is not my specialty.

This town was my home for eighteen long years, and on days like today, I remember why I was so anxious to leave. Before this visit, I had spent a lot of time considering its details: the charming streets, slower life, proximity to the beach, quality time spent with family. I was convinced this place was what I wanted. Now that I've arrived, the days drag. Arguing with my mother seems to be the only activity that breaks the monotony.

In Toronto, most of my close friends are now busy parents of little ones, while other friends have moved away from the city. These changes have me wondering whether moving on and away is something I want too. A successful job and a fear of missing out have been hard to let go of, but my decision to stay city-bound is slowly eroding my happiness the way wind and water erode the cliffs circling Lake Erie.

Despite my uncertainty about the future, I had been confident I was homesick. For what, I didn't know, so I went home to see if it might solve my persistent longing.

I open the creaking gate and exit the backyard, then set my pace to high speed—but there's no need to rush here. I'm not in downtown Toronto competing for sidewalk space or racing to the subway to be on time for work. I slow down, trying to enjoy the feeling of my body in motion. The stress that often accompanies me while I'm walking in the city dissipates. Green scents sail into my lungs, and together they swell like the waves of nearby Lake Erie in a storm.

I turn my thoughts to my feet. The sidewalks here buck and heave like horses at a rodeo, and sprays of weeds adorn the concrete cracks. Shadows of leaves shuffle in the breeze, cast by yellow streetlights dotting narrow roads. I peek into the sky and see stars, even in the town proper. Tension leaks from my shoulders.

I come upon Smith's, the local convenience store, and am teleported to my youth. People still congregate here for evening ice cream, forever devoted to the local dairy company that has a monopoly in these parts. I don't mind the monopoly—the ice cream is quite good.

I watch as families gather and talk with friends met by chance at this well-known establishment. The tradition extends to the local Mennonite community, and I glimpse several Mennonite families who have parked their horses and buggies under trees that skirt the parking lot. As I observe the friendly conversations, I miss the sense of being known, of being able to easily meet up with the people in my life. I startle out of my sentiments as white floodlights switch on, illuminating the parking lot and patrons. The last of the day has been washed from the sky, and I blink to help my pupils adjust to the bright light.

I resume my meandering stroll, but look back when a deep voice shouts my name. I frown, not recognizing the low cadence, and twist to see a man walking quickly towards me. He is eating his cone in the sort of big bites that would zing my teeth and cause my forehead to freeze.

"I didn't know you were in town!" exclaims the man. I squint at him as the floodlights halo his head, casting shadows over his face and making it difficult to puzzle out.

I nod, smiling vacantly, and wonder why I would ever tell this mystery man I was in the area.

He pauses, self-consciously running a hand through the fawn-coloured hair curling about his brow. The movement is so familiar, I am certain I know him. I tilt my head like a dog hearing its name, and look into his eyes, trying to discern who is before me.

"Oh, uh. It's me—" he starts, but then I finish his sentence: "*Derek!*"

He laughs with relief, and then begins to walk in the direction I'm heading. I question whether I want this almost-stranger along for my evening stroll but being straightforward with others has never been a strength of mine. Besides, there is something I implicitly trust about this man I haven't seen in twenty years. Nevertheless, I finger the pepper spray in my bag to confirm it's within reach. I will never confide this to my mother.

I fall in step, recalling the younger Derek as being an awkward friend of a friend. Now he is all grown up and looking all the better for it.

"What brings you here, Nat?" he asks conversationally. "Last I heard, you were never coming back." His eyes shift to look at me, and then away.

It isn't a secret that Mom had a hip replacement, so I tell him about her surgery and my role as daughter-helper-chef-cleaner-nurse-physiotherapist while she heals. I talk about how I work my nine-to-five out of her wood-panelled basement, taking Zoom video meetings when necessary, hiding the dated walls with various virtual backgrounds.

"It isn't perfect. She's not an easy one to live with," I admit with uncharacteristic honesty. "But there are times when I like being here with her, back in this little town. There's something nice about it—something comforting."

I think about the repetitive arguments we have—Dad's calming presence no longer around to take the combative edge from our interactions—and that I struggle to like the person I become when I'm here too long.

Belatedly, I ask about his life. "And you? What are you doing taking up residence here? I heard you had moved to Montreal for some huge job?"

"Ah, yes. That." He smiles, but there is pain around his eyes when I glance at him.

"I ended up moving back home. Jess left me, and everything in Montreal reminded me of her. It didn't help that most of my friends had been her friends first, and people took sides. It got lonely. So, I phoned my mom and here I am: 38 years old and living in her basement." Derek says this last part ruefully, a broad smile fracturing his face.

I nod sympathetically before asking, "You think you'll stay?" I am genuinely curious about Derek's impending life choices, fascinated that he's opted for the path back to living in this place.

Derek is silent for so long, I think he hasn't heard me. I jump when he next speaks.

"Undecided." He sighs good-naturedly. "It hasn't been

terrible. Everyone thinks you're supposed to understand who you are and what you'll be by this stage in life. But I don't know anymore. I'm not sure I ever did. It's not a bad realization—it's sort of exciting." His mouth gently rises at the corners like dough in the oven. I wait, but even after a few minutes, he doesn't add anything.

"I get that," I admit. "I don't know what I'm doing either."

I say this in a too-neutral voice because I am struggling with the truth. Toronto isn't as great as it used to be, and I miss my mom now that she is in her twilight years—even though she sometimes steps on every nerve I have. I keep hesitating to make a change, because I don't know if I can, or where I belong. Walking past groups of people socializing at the local ice cream haunt is the loveliest thing I've seen in a long time.

"Life's hard, you know?" he says as if in response to the strife within me, his face alternating between light and shadow from the flickering lamp posts as we walk. We aren't acquainted with each other well enough to go much deeper than this worn universal sentiment. But I nod. Because it is.

I sneak a sidelong look at Derek, and marvel at all the shifts he's made in his life. He's survived an encounter with real hardship, a move across provinces—and persevered.

Derek's proven it doesn't have to be too late to start over.

My stomach leaps at the thought of change, and I can't tell if it's bouncing with horror or excitement, but the feeling is not altogether unpleasant.

"Do you remember that time we all rode in Stan's car

with the windows down, blaring "Life Is a Highway" into the countryside? And then we ended up at the beach and went skinny-dipping?" Derek's grin is wide, and it is the grin I remember from our teenage years. The impish one that makes his eyes sparkle with real mirth.

I startle at this memory, only now recalling that this carefree night of road trips and skinny-dips existed. I laugh in delight, my mind filling in the blanks, and I am back at the moonlit shores of Lake Erie with hundreds of fishflies gathered at the water's edge. I remember screaming as they landed on my bare skin. We raced to the lake to avoid them perching on every inch of our bodies, diving in to rinse them away.

"And remember when we went cliff diving?"

"You have a great memory!" I chuckle. "We were so fearless!"

"And maybe sometimes a bit reckless?" Derek pinches his pointer finger and thumb together, laughing.

Affection blooms in my chest for the younger me, when I felt free and flung myself from cliff faces. When I propelled myself into the future without apprehension.

Abruptly, I'm homesick again, and for a moment, I can't quite put my finger on for what or for whom.

I have the strange sensation that my mind is the combination lock to a safe that is in the process of being opened: cogs shifting and moving to release the locking mechanism, door swinging out to display what's inside.

What do I find? I am homesick for *me*.

Not the person I now become when I argue with my

mother, but a truer, older version of myself.

It's a joy to meet her again.

Derek stops and lingers in front of an asphalt driveway that leads to a white-sided house. "Thanks for walking me home," he jokes. "I'd offer to walk *you* home, but I think you seem more than capable of taking care of yourself on these mean streets."

I nod, and experience real pleasure at having run into him—at Smith's, no less. "Good to see you," I say, and I mean it. "I might look you up sometime before I leave."

I turn and go, leaving him to the rest of his evening, and maybe to the rest of his life. I don't think I could ever move back here like Derek, but for the time being, I am pulled to return to my temporary home at my mother's. I know something is waiting there for me, so I turn on my walking-in-Toronto speed.

When I slow in front of the old 1970s bungalow, the living room lights gleam warmly through the windows, and it occurs to me what all those flies must see when they dash into my mother's house: a sanctuary and a place to land—even if a temporary and ill-suited one.

My heart thwaps against my rib cage as I step through Mom's front door, an epiphany shining, clear as her polished glass panes.

I don't have to be stuck on the wrong side of the glass. And I'm no longer afraid of what's waiting for me because I've done this before.

There, in my mother's kitchen, my heart gathers for the leap before running towards the ledge, my legs kicking free in the air of my imagination. I'm free-falling into my unknowable future.

It's exhilarating.

LULU, QUEEN STREET, PIES, AND AUGUST VS. SAUL, SUZANNA, A CHICKEN BUNGALOW, AND NOVEMBER

Karen Walker

Irises

ULU AND SAUL BLOOMED AMONG THE IRISES one summer night in Precious Corners.

The next morning, Lulu told her Townie girlfriends about it. How Saul had pulled off his Ralph Lauren sweater and laid her on it, how he later found her bra. And that the rumours—long dished by Townies in the darkest booths of Patsy's Tea Room—were wrong. So wrong, Lulu told her girlfriends. Big Cit men were not all weedy, not all limp and ineffectual.

Wow!

"Yeah, they act like big fish in a small pond, but that's a good thing down in my garden," she giggled. "Look at me giggling after menopause!"

The women laughed.

"I hope he'll kiss and tell," said Lulu because mean things circulated at the Precious Corners Yacht Club and other places where Big Cits like Saul gathered. Things about Townie gals, that they were unkempt and as frigid as November.

The women cheered Lulu.

Lulu and Saul made love in the well-tended flower beds behind her red brick bungalow.

Saul, a recently retired CEO, had bought the cottage next door. He demolished it, erecting a steel and glass ice cube of a house over the ruins. Then he felled a century-old oak in the backyard and xeriscaped with white gravel and agave.

Lulu was on her knees weeding as the great tree toppled.

Saul saw her there, said: "Madam, it simply doesn't fit my vision. There is no need for prayer."

"Damn your big city vision!" Lulu pointed to a heaven of colourful irises. "That oak shaded my beauties from the scorching afternoon sun." She hurled clods of soil and foul words at him.

Suddenly—its frilly tongue petals coated with sawdust—a miniature blue iris began to choke. Lulu leapt to the tallest of her tall varieties and cradled the stricken plant in her hands.

Before she could scream, Saul was at her side. He pulled

a monogrammed handkerchief from the pocket of his khakis, gently wiped away the sawdust. The plant quickly recovered.

Whew.

Saul dabbed Lulu's tears with the sleeve of his pricey sweater. "I'd like to get to know your irises, madam."

And he did, shoving aside his white gravel and digging flowerbeds. The agave, though they were miffed, minded their thorns.

Lulu transplanted iris rhizomes from her garden into his. She told the man he'd have to be patient: there probably wouldn't be blooms until next year.

Saul wilted. Lulu smiled at his sad face. "Honey, I won't take so long."

And she didn't. On the torrid night, before Townie and Big Cit came together and flowered, she sat very close to Saul as they kept watch for iris borer.

"The bug chews the heart of a plant," Lulu said, fingers crawling up his leg.

"Wicked thing," Saul whispered and kissed her.

Queen Street

It was Suzanna's first descent of Queen Street on this, her second day in Precious Corners.

She began with tiny halting steps then, gaining speed down the awful hill, grabbed tree after tree, pole after pole, and cursed and cursed Jim the real estate agent. "I'd like to push the bastard."

On a warm evening in June, he had sold her 244 Queen Street and sold her on easy small-town living. No more city stress. Lost in the fog and the idyll of the place, she believed him when he promised everything was just a gentle stroll down the hill.

Arms and legs flailing, Suzanna came to a stop at the foot of Queen. She looked back up and swore. Swore as she shopped at downtown Precious Corners' little supermarket and its big dollar store. Swore as she plopped on a bench outside the pawnshop.

A passerby heard her cussing and saw her bulging shopping bags.

"Take the bus," suggested the Townie. "The Queen is cruel, eh?"

Halfway up the mountain, where a deli stood like a base camp, Suzanna's legs faltered. They pleaded to stop. *Bus, bus!* Her heart pounded. *No more. Call an Uber.* And Suzanna's hands failed her too, shaking so badly the phone fell to the sidewalk and skidded away down Queen Street.

A clerk saw it go. The boy yelled for someone below to catch it. People scrambled, but like a panicked chicken, the phone scooted between feet and into the street, and was crunched by the town bus.

"Fuck! Call me a ride," she snapped before remembering where she was. "Please." The clerk said he was sorry for her loss, then: "My Uncle Stan drives for A-1 Taxi."

As the cab chugged up, up, up Queen Street, Suzanna gasped in the back seat and had no air to swear when Stan asked: "Hey, didn't my cousin Jim sell ya a house?"

The Ed Bogg Fog

This is the fog, the fog rising off Lake Ontario and rolling over The Lakeview Condos at nightfall. The fog Townies still call The Ed Bogg Fog. The Ed Bogg who lived in Precious Corners long ago and who, many said, must've been in a fog of his own when, swatting mosquitoes, he rolled out plans for the town's swampy lakeshore. "Drain it," Ed Bogg exclaimed. "Rake the beach. Build quaint tourist cabins." This is the fog that wasn't there when Ed took photographs and sent them to a glossy magazine in the city, the fog that did, however, soon notice many summer visitors. Visitors who said: "What a pretty town, what a pretty beach. Let's rent the cabins and boost the local economy." The same fog that, sixty years later, watched swanky condos rise where the cabins had stood. The fog now rapping on a fourth-floor balcony door to summon a Big Cit named Catharine. The Catharine who overpaid for a 850 sq. ft. two bath and one bedroom unit, who always overpaid a city salon to style her hair. Her straight, flat hair. Hair that the fog now winds around misty fingers, creating body and bounce without spray, rollers, or mousse. The fog that rolls its grey eyes when Catharine forgets where she is, what it is, and starts calling it Roz—her old stylist in the city.

The Girls

Old Lucien hugged each chicken before putting it into the cage.

Young Lydia hid a smile behind her hand, shuffled her Jimmy Choo booties.

"The buff hen is bossy Hyacinth," said the scruffy little farmer. "There's white Daisy and Rose. Violet is the big reddish-brown one."

Lydia clucked: "So sweet."

"Ever watch *Keeping Up Appearances*?" Lucien asked.

The woman shook her head.

"Damn funny Brit show. I named the girls after the sisters in it."

Ignoring him, Lydia cooed to the birds. "Hello there. Go for a ride?" She dangled the keys of her shiny Mercedes SUV in front of the cage.

Humph. "Watch it sometime," he snorted. "All about being hoity-toity."

Though Lydia smiled, Lucien felt he shouldn't have said it. *Nice of a Big Cit to be interested in old-fashioned things like chickens.*

He told her the hens were chantecler, a hardy old Canadian breed. Good layers and good mums if left to go broody.

"Going broody means hatching eggs, right?"

"Right. You'll make a good Townie."

Lydia mumbled how kind, that he was sweet too.

"Find them a nice boy if ya want chicks," Lucien explained, warming. "They don't need him around just for eggs."

"Oh, I had an argument over this with my partner, Arturo. Mr. Know-It-All said they did."

Pfft. "Just like a Big Cit, eh?" The farmer winced. *Damn big mouth.* "Apologies, my dear. I'm, I'm about to turn into a Big Cit myself."

When he had toured Blue Pines Seniors' Residence in the city, Lucien hadn't seen any pine trees. Blue or otherwise. Still, there were gardens. They were nice. The room was okay and the complimentary lunch in the dining room tasty enough. The place was, his son assured him, only twenty minutes from his place. Traffic permitting.

"*Mon Dieu*, who would've thought it?" Lucien looked past the woman, into the golden summer sunset. One of the last nights on his farm was beginning.

"We're both making new starts. Me here and you where I was. I didn't live far from Blue Pines," Lydia replied. "Sorry to tell you traffic is always bad."

Lucien rubbed his stubble and said quietly: "Never mind me." Then, like a bantam rooster protecting his flock: "Will the girls have a nice coop?"

On Lydia's phone was a photo of The Bungalow, the deluxe chicken house she had purchased online. Lucien chuckled. He grinned at the all-cedar construction, at the two-level interior with removable floor trays for easy cleaning. He nodded approval at the cozy nesting boxes with hinged lids, at the ventilation doors with bug screens. And, in spite of himself, he cackled at the skylight, roared at the striped awning over the attached fenced yard, and at the exterior stain—a shade called Rhode Island Red—Lydia had chosen instead of siding.

Lucien wiped his eyes. "I might move in too."

Most Precious Pie

A poster on the library bulletin board amused Arturo.

"Enter the 9th Annual New Friends Church Pie Contest" it proclaimed from on high, pinned as it was near the top of the board. A man with a long white beard—known to many, though not to Arturo, as Reverend Moses Beamish—held two tablets inscribed with the rules:

1. The contest is open to all. We are glad you have joined us.
2. Registration is 3 to 6 p.m. on Saturday, July 25 at the church hall. Judging at 7 sharp.
3. Bakers may enter one or more of the following categories: raspberry, cherry, peach.
4. The pie judged to be the best in each category will compete for Most Precious Pie.
5. Baking supplies and ingredients must be purchased locally. Bring receipts for verification. Visit Beamish's Grocery for everything you need, including quality produce from the Lloyd Fruit Farm. Raspberries, cherries, and peaches now in season.
6. $25 entry fee per pie or $30 with a charitable tax receipt. Cash only. Payable at Sunday services.
7. The baker's name must accompany each pie.
8. The decisions of the New Friends Church judges (Reverend Beamish, Mrs. Muriel

Beamish, Ladies Auxiliary Chair Patsy Beamish Lloyd, and Treasurer Sam Lloyd) are final.

9. Prizes will be gift certificates generously donated by the Lloyd Fruit Farm, Patsy's Tea Room, and Beamish's Grocery.

10. Winning pies become the property of the judges. Pie dishes can be claimed by calling Muriel, but donations to the church kitchen are appreciated. Put a big X through your name if you do not wish to help and want your dish back.

Below these commandments was a flirty pie in high heels welcoming all to Patsy's Tea Room after the contest. Come enjoy a slice of winning pie. $7.50 per person.

Arturo ripped the poster from the bulletin board. He stuffed it into his pocket. "This looks fun," said the accomplished Big Cit baker. "But to hell with all the church crap."

November

Lulu kept track on a calendar from Beamish's Grocery.

In August, Saul visited twenty-five times. Humidity remained high, and they made love twenty-two times. Indoors though: several iris leaves and at least one flower stalk had been damaged during that evening in the garden. The winds being light and southerly, Lulu forecast a forever with Saul.

In September, thirteen visits and seven love-makings. Most occurred early in the month, there being a definite cooling trend by the first day of autumn. Saul got dressed and left earlier and earlier, refusing Lulu's late night offers of pie and more iris rhizomes.

Temperature and barometric pressure dropped dramatically in October: just two visits, no love at all. Lulu didn't count— in fact, she rebuffed—his bumbling on a Sunday afternoon after she found him drunk at the Precious Corners Yacht Club. Other Big Cits were there. They stared at her and elbowed each other. They sniggered hurtful things about Townies, rumours Lulu expected Saul to squash like iris borers. But he didn't. He laughed along with his buddies.

The winds of November came from the west, as the man himself had. They brought short, dark days and the first snow to Precious Corners. They caused Lulu to make new marks on the calendar—angry red Xs for each of her many calls and texts to Saul: "The growing season is over" and "Have ya tucked your irises into bed?"

He never answered, never tended to his shivering babes. Lulu hilled mulch around them. She hushed their cries of "Where's Papa?"

One particularly bitter day, Lulu pounded on Saul's fancy etched glass door with a frozen muddy fist. Shocked she was when a young woman appeared. A house-sitter! Saul having left for Palm Beach! Not back until April!

"He didn't say the gardener would be around," the woman said to Lulu with a shrug. "Sorry, but I can't pay you right now."

ABOUT THE AUTHORS

Crystal Randall Barnett (pg. 63) lives in Waterloo, Ontario with her partner, her dog, and her disability, Post-Concussion Syndrome. She studied rhetoric and professional writing at the University of Waterloo and has a Master of Education from the University of Toronto. Crystal's work has been published by *Blank Spaces, Writerly Magazine*, and The League of Canadian Poets. She adores reading, Earl Grey tea, and being in nature—often at the same time.

Daryl Bruce (he/him) (pg. 21) is a recovering dairy farmer turned writer based in Montreal, Quebec. An emerging voice in queer Canadian prose and poetry, his work has appeared in *The Antigonish Review, Open Minds Quarterly,* and more. Chronically over-caffeinated, he is currently working on his masters at Concordia University.

Finnian Burnett (pg. 29) teaches undergrad English and creative writing. They've published with *Reflex Press, Bath Flash, Ekphrastic Review, the Daily Science Fiction*, and more. Finn's novella-in-flash, *The Clothes Make the Man*, recently released through AdHoc Fiction, and their second novella, *The Price of Cookies*, is forthcoming through Off Topic Publishing. In their spare time, Finnian Burnett watches a lot of *Star Trek* and takes their cat for long walks in a stroller. Finn lives in British Columbia, with their wife and Lord Gordo, the cat. Finn can be found at www.finnburnett.com.

Alyssa Bushell (pg. 3) lives and writes at the shore of Lake Huron in southern Ontario. Alyssa's work appears in *Ellipsis Zine, Reckon Review,* and *Leon Literary Review,* among other online and print publications. She is currently working on her debut mystery novel and can often be found baking up new ways to procrastinate. Find her at: @WritesAly or AlyWrites.ca.

Casey Fehr (pg. 9) has always stayed up way too late reading with a flashlight under the covers. Her love of reading has naturally expanded to include writing the type of stories that she would like to read. She is an elementary school teacher in British Columbia and loves dogs, tea, and travel.

Jennifer Moffatt (pg. 51) lives with her family in British Columbia, and enjoys writing stories about diverse people falling in love. She is working on her second novel and can be found on Twitter @JMoffattWrites.

Noa Padawer-Blatt (pg. 37) is a writer and poet from Toronto, Ontario. She currently resides in Montreal, where she studies English and film as an undergraduate at McGill University. Her work can be found in *carte blanche, Blue Marble Review,* and *Synaesthesia Magazine.*

Karen Walker (pg. 75) writes very short fiction in Ontario. Her work is in or forthcoming in *FlashBack Fiction, The Disappointed Housewife, Reflex Fiction, Versification, Virtual Zine, Ghost City Press, The Ekphrastic Review*, and others. (she/her) @MeKawalker883.

Other Canadian Short Story Anthologies
from Chicken House Press:

The Things We Leave Behind (2022)

Manufactured by Amazon.ca
Bolton, ON

33670121R00059